Coyote Places
the Stars

Retold and illustrated by

Harriet Peck Taylor

Aladdin Paperbacks

First Aladdin Paperbacks edition May 1997
Text copyright © 1993 by Harriet Peck Taylor
Illustrations © 1993 by Harriet Peck Taylor

Aladdin Paperbacks
An imprint of Simon & Schuster Children's Publishing Division
1230 Avenue of the Americas, New York, NY 10020

Also available in a Simon & Schuster Books for Young Readers edition
The text of this book was set in 16-point Goudy Old Style.
Manufactured in China
30

The Library of Congress has cataloged the hardcover edition as follows:
Taylor, Harriet Peck.
Coyote places the stars / retold and illustrated by Harriet Peck Taylor. — 1st ed.
p.   cm.
Summary: Coyote arranges the stars in the shapes of his animal friends.
ISBN 978-0-02-788845-4
1. Wasco Indians—Legends.   2. Coyote (Legendary character)   3. Constellations—
Folklore.   [1. Wasco Indians—Legends.   2. Indians of North America—Legends.
3. Coyote (Legendary character)   4. Constellations—Folklore.]   I. Title.
E99.W37P43 1993
398.2—dc20
[E]   92-46431

ISBN 978-0-689-81535-5 (Aladdin pbk.)

0918 SCP

*To stargazers everywhere,
and to their dreams*

Many moons and many moons ago, a coyote lived in a canyon by a swift-running river. He spent his days roaming the land, chasing butterflies and sniffing wildflowers. He lay awake many nights gazing at the starry heavens.

One summer night, as he was relaxing in the cool grass with his friend Bear, Coyote had an idea. "I think I will climb to the heavens and discover their secrets!"

Bear scratched his big head and asked, "How can you do that?"

"I can get up there with no trouble at all," Coyote said.

Now, Coyote was very skillful with a bow and arrow. He gathered a very large pile of arrows and began to shoot them at the sky. The first arrow whistled through the air and landed on the moon. Coyote launched a second arrow, which caught in the notch of the first. *Whi-rr* went one arrow. *Whizz* went the next, and on and on until this long line of arrows made a ladder.

Coyote then began to climb. He climbed for many days and nights until he finally reached the moon. He slept all that day, as he was very tired.

That night Coyote had another clever idea. He wondered if he could move the stars around by shooting at them with his remaining arrows. His first arrow hit a star and moved it across the sky. He found he could place the stars wherever he wanted.

Coyote wagged his bushy tail and yelped for joy. He was going to make pictures in the sky for all the world to see.

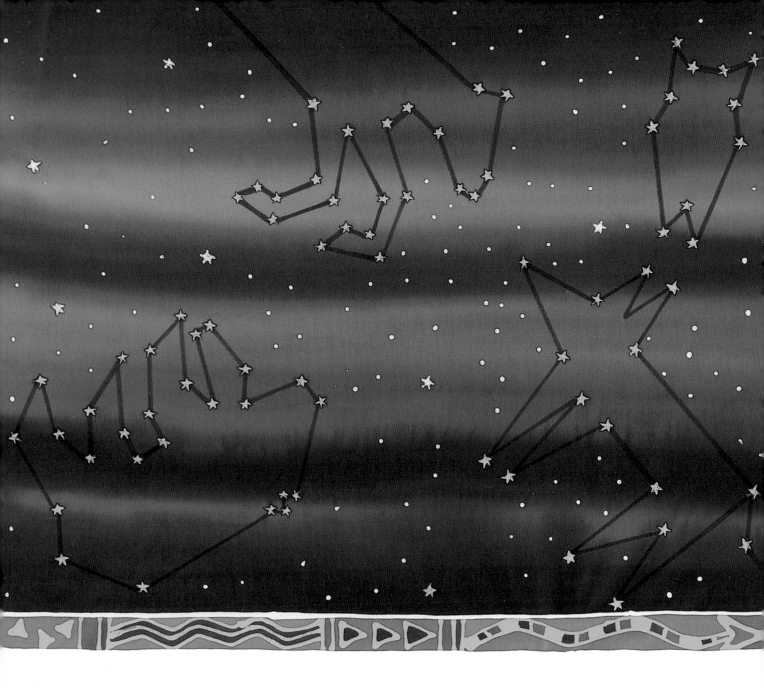

First he decided to make a coyote, so he shot one
arrow after another until the stars were arranged in the
shape of a coyote. Next he thought of his friend Bear,
and placed the stars in the form of a bear.

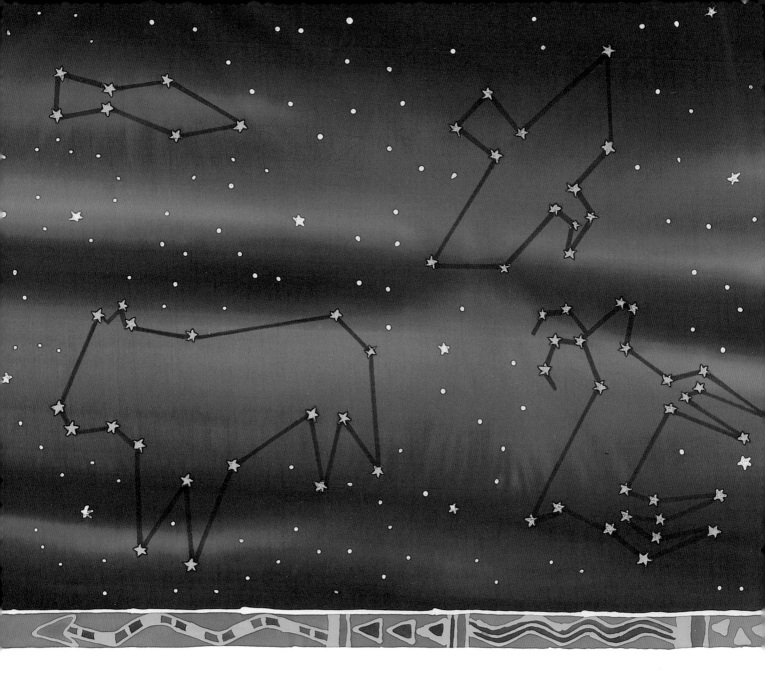

Coyote worked all night creating likenesses of all his
friends—Mountain Lion, Horse, Goat, Fish, Owl, and
Eagle. With the stars he had left over, he made a Big
Road across the sky. When he was finished, he began
to descend his ladder back to earth.

That night, when the bright moon rose in the east, Coyote saw his handiwork and began to howl. *Oweowowooooah* was carried on the wind through the shadows of the canyon. Birds and animals awoke suddenly and listened to the mysterious sound. It seemed to be calling to them. From canyons and mesas, hills and plains they came, following the sound.

Bears bounded out of their dens. Squirrels scampered
and rabbits hippity-hopped over the hills. Bobcats crept
and bristly porcupines waddled along the trail.

Graceful deer moved swiftly, while lizards slowly crawled across the desert.

Silvery fish splashed their way upstream. The mighty
mountain lion and herds of buffalo joined the journey.

The great eagle soared over moonlit mountains. On and on went the parade of animals, following Coyote's magical voice.

Finally Coyote appeared, high on a rock. The animals formed a huge circle and all became quiet. Coyote's eyes blazed with pride as he said, "Animals and birds and all who are gathered here: Please look at the sky. You will see the stars are arranged in the shapes of animals. I made a ladder to the moon, and from there I shot my arrows to create the pictures you see."

As the animals looked up, a great chorus of whoofing and whiffing, screeching and squawking filled the air.

"I made a coyote and my friend Bear. You will see the mysterious Owl, the great Eagle, the Goat, Horse, Fish, and the mighty Mountain Lion. This is my handiwork, and I hope that all who see it will remember Coyote and all the animals of the canyon."

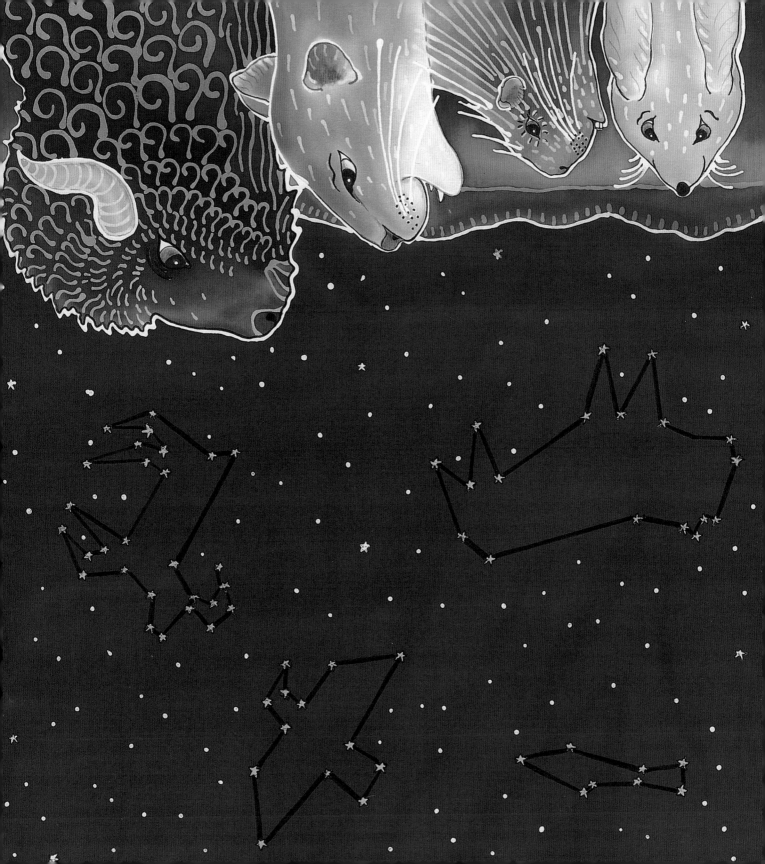

The animals gave a great feast for Coyote, and they sang and danced through the night. The animals decreed that Coyote was the most clever and crafty of all the animals.

Coyote was so grateful that he declared, "I will always be your friend and the friend of your children's children."

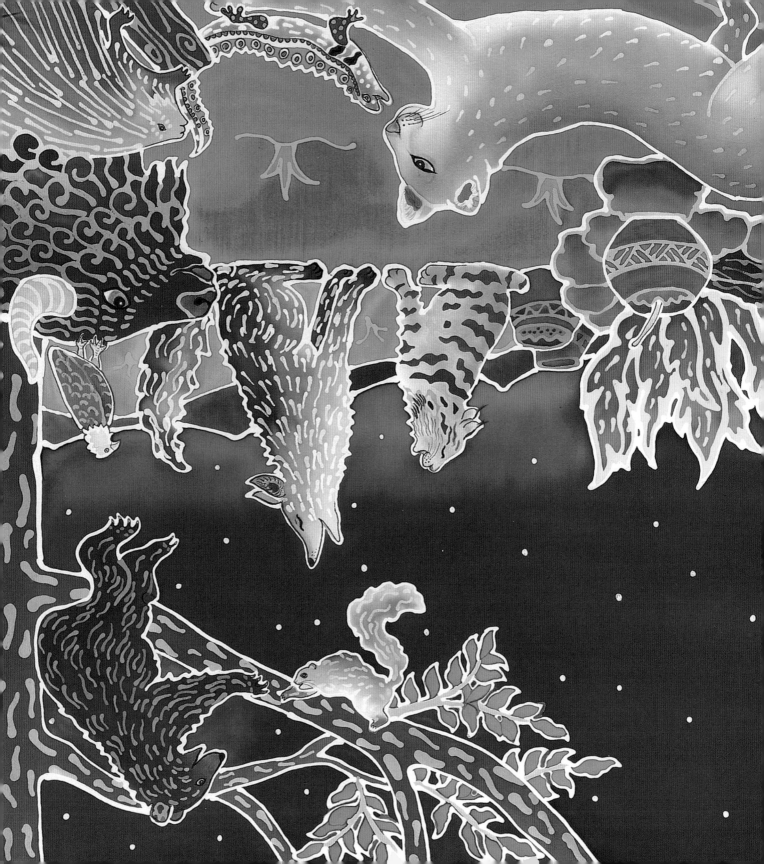

Now, to this day, if you listen closely in the still of the night as the moon is rising, you may even hear the magical howl of Coyote. He is calling you to go to your window, to gaze at the star pictures, and to dream.

Coyote Places the Stars, a retelling of a Wasco Indian story, is based on two printed versions of the legend: "How Coyote Arranged the Night Sky" in *They Dance in the Sky: Native American Star Myths* by Jean Guard Monroe and Ray A. Williamson (New York: Houghton Mifflin, 1987) and "Coyote Places the Stars" in *Giving Birth to Thunder Sleeping with His Daughter: Coyote Builds North America* by Barry Holstun Lopez (Kansas City: Sheed, Andrews and McMeel, 1977).

To create the illustrations, the artist painted with dyes on cotton fabric. Detailing was applied in a wax-resist batik method. Transparencies of the art were then color-separated using four-color process.

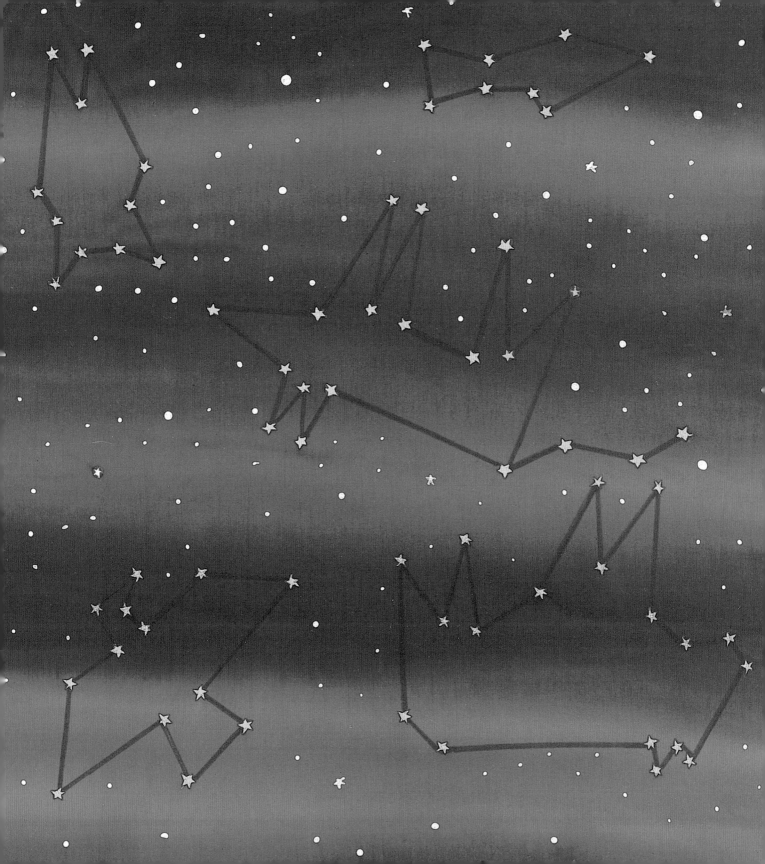

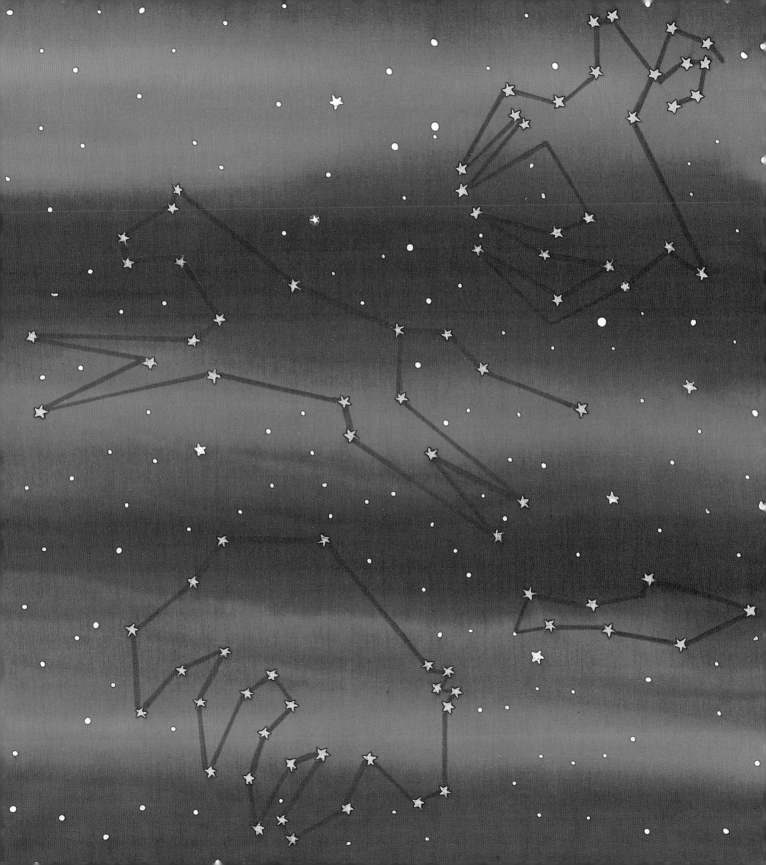